Raffi Songs to Read®

FIVE LITTLE DUCKS

Illustrated by Jose Aruego and Ariane Dewey

Crown Publishers, New York

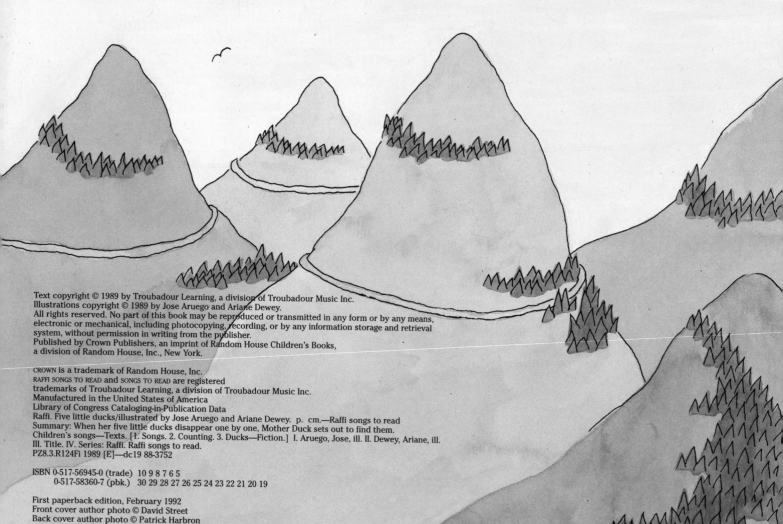

Published by Crown Publishers, an imprint of Random House Children's Books,
a division of Random House, Inc., New York.

CROWN is a trademark of Random House, Inc.
RAFFI SONGS TO READ and SONGS TO READ are registered
trademarks of Troubadour Learning, a division of Troubadour Music Inc.
Manufactured in the United States of America
Library of Congress Cataloging-in-Publication Data
Raffi. Five little ducks/illustrated by Jose Aruego and Ariane Dewey. p. cm.—Raffi songs to read
Summary: When her five little ducks disappear one by one, Mother Duck sets out to find them.
Children's songs—Texts. [1. Songs. 2. Counting. 3. Ducks—Fiction.] I. Aruego, Jose, ill. II. Dewey, Ariane, ill.
III. Title. IV. Series: Raffi. Raffi songs to read.
PZ8.3.R124Fi 1989 [E]—dc19 88-3752

ISBN 0-517-56945-0 (trade) 10 9 8 7 6 5
     0-517-58360-7 (pbk.)   30 29 28 27 26 25 24 23 22 21 20 19

First paperback edition, February 1992
Front cover author photo © David Street
Back cover author photo © Patrick Harbron

Five little ducks went out one day,
Over the hills and far away.

Mother Duck said,
"Quack, quack, quack, quack."

But only four little ducks came back.

Four little ducks went out one day,
Over the hills and far away.

Mother Duck said,
"Quack, quack, quack, quack."

But only three little ducks came back.

Three little ducks went out one day,
Over the hills and far away.

Mother Duck said,
"Quack, quack, quack, quack."

But only two little ducks came back.

Two little ducks went out one day,
Over the hills and far away.

Mother Duck said,
"Quack, quack, quack, quack."

But only one little duck came back.

One little duck went out one day,
Over the hills and far away.

Mother Duck said,
"Quack, quack, quack, quack."

But none of the five little ducks came back.

Sad Mother Duck went out one day,
Over the hills and far away.

Mother Duck said, "Quack, quack, quack, quack!"

And all of the five little ducks came back.

FIVE LITTLE DUCKS

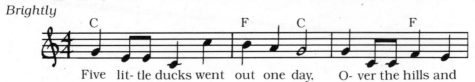

Brightly

Five lit-tle ducks went out one day, O- ver the hills and

far a- way. Mo- ther duck said, "Quack, quack, quack, quack!" But

on- ly four lit- tle ducks came back.

2. Four little ducks went out one day...
   But only three little ducks came back.

3. Three little ducks went out one day...
   But only two little ducks came back.

4. Two little ducks went out one day...
   But only one little duck came back.

5. One little duck went out one day...
   But none of the five little ducks came back.

6. Sad mother duck went out one day...
   And all of the five little ducks came back.

5264